Our Little Feudal Cousin of Long Ago

This edition published 2026
by Living Book Press

ISBN: 978-1-76183-125-6 (hardcover)
         978-1-76183-143-0 (softcover)

First published in 1913 as *The Little Master*.

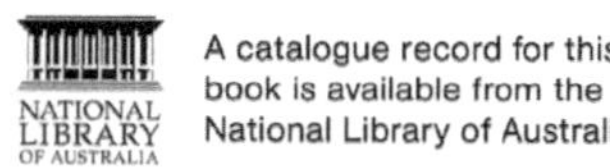

Our Little Feudal Cousin of Long Ago

by

Laura Elizabeth Howe Richards

Contents

"'Tis a Doo Pasty!' she cried."

PREFACE

THIS little book was published some years ago under the title of "The Little Master," and was intended, as the dedication tells, as a key to the great gate that leads to "the ballad country." It is thought now that Alan Gordon and his sister Elspat may well join the company of Little Cousins of Long Ago with whom so many of our young people are making acquaintance. They certainly are our cousins, not in common humanity alone, but in blood and race, for we Americans, of English descent, claim near kinship with the Scots, and their traditions run side by side with ours. Especially is this the case with the old ballads, many of which are found, in different versions, on either side of the Border between England and Scotland. The minstrels, making their way from house to house, from castle to castle, had friends in every part of the country. In those days, when books were few, and none — as a rule — could read except the priests, the minstrel and his harp were eagerly welcomed by high and low. They wove into simple rhyme the wild doings, the wilder legends, of the countryside, Highland, Lowland, or Saxon; and recited them, or sang to the wild, sweet music of their harps, while the hearers listened spellbound, often calling for a favorite ballad over and over till they knew it by heart, and so made it their own. It is to the minstrels that we owe much of our knowledge of old times in England and Scotland.

The following pages tell in simple fashion of the life of a Scottish boy and girl in the fourteenth century, and of how David the harper helped them in their hour of need.

April 12, 1922.

CHAPTER I

LONG AGO AND LONG AGO

LONG ago and long ago, in the Lowlands of Scotland, lived a boy just about your age, who was called the Little Master. He had another name, and that was Alan Gordon; he was the son of a great Baron, and Master[1] was the title that belonged to him. It was a castle that he lived in, great and gray and old, with winding stone staircases, and queer narrow windows, and lofty turrets; yes, it was exactly like the pictures of castles in the story-books. You see, the pictures were made from real castles, not the other way. There the Little Master lived, with his father the Lord, and his mother the Lady, and his sister the Lady Elspat. These were the principal people, but there were many others in the castle, and every one of them his friend. There was the old nurse, Oona, who had been the Baron's nurse when he was little, and who was now so old and white that she was more like a white shadow than a real woman, and yet so kind and dear that one loved to be with her; and there

1   Master. In Scotland, the title of the eldest son of a viscount or baron.

was Duncan the steward, her son, himself an old man; and there was John the smith, and Donald the falconer, and Leezie the dairymaid, and a dozen more of them, young and old. And beside these was David Johnstone, the harper. David did not live in the castle; he wandered about the country with his harp, staying a night here and a night there, welcome wherever he went for the sake of his kindly face, the sweetness of his voice and harp, and the songs he sang.

All these people the Little Master loved, first for themselves, because they loved him and were kind to him; secondly, for the stories they told and the songs they sang. For the Little Master, and little Lady Elspat, who was about your little sister's age, loved songs and stories just as much as you do, and perhaps a good deal more; and they had no story-books: think of that! There were no books at all in the great old castle, and if there had been no one could have read them except Father Neil, the chaplain. I forgot Father Neil in my list of the Little Master's friends, and that was a sad forgetting, for he was one of the best of them, and knew some of the very best stories of all. But, as I was saying, no one else could have read books if there had been any. Those were wild, rude times, long ago and long ago. Very few people could read or write, and the Baron thought it a foolish and an unmanly thing for a man to be seen poring over a written page. (There were no printed books in those days.)

Knotting a man's brains into cobwebs! he would say, when Father Neil would beg to be allowed to teach the Little Master to read and write. Not for my son! Set him on a horse, and let him ride till he drops asleep in the saddle; so shall we make a man of him, not with moth-eaten parchment scrawled with foolish signs.

All the same, the Little Master wished to learn, and hoped some day to persuade his father to allow it; but now he must be content with stories; and as I said, he heard many and many of them; for all the Scottish people loved stories, too, and do to this day; and in the want of books they stored their brains with tales and ballads, grave and gay, gentle and savage: of Border rides, fights, escapes, brave deeds of rescue and heroism, cruel deeds of blood and revenge. All these the two children, Alan and Elspat, used to hear, over and over, till they knew them by heart; and then they liked them all the better, because if Oona or Duncan or David made a mistake of a single word they could correct it, and that was a pleasant thing to do.

Suppose it was the story of Kempion that old Oona

was telling, as she sat at her spinning-wheel, twirling the white flax in her fingers.

They would be sitting on the wide landing at the head of the great stone staircase; all three close in the corner, to be out of the cold blast that whistled up the stairs; Alan on his three-legged stool (he called it a creepie); Elspat on the pretty little low cricket that Tam the joiner made for her, of walnut wood, with a wreath of daisies carved round it. The little girl wore a short frock of homespun cloth, or in summer of linen; wool and linen alike were spun by old Oona, and woven by the Lady and her maids at the looms that stood in the great stone workroom; but the boy's frock or tunic was of soft leather, with a leather belt round it, and wooden buttons, carved by the same skilful Tam, into the likeness of animal's heads: a dog, a horse, a wolf, and a fox. Alan wanted a stag, but Tam said no, the horns would break too easily, and his buttons were to last him all his life.

And what were the children like, inside these quaint clothes? Why, the Little Master was brown like his own coat, from running in sun and wind. His hair was brown too, and his eyes like dark diamonds. He could run like a hare, and whistle like a blackbird; he rode his pony bareback, and he was learning to shoot straight and far.

Oona, Alan and Elspat.

For the rest of him, you shall see for yourself what kind of boy he was.

And little Elspat was just a posy out of a garden, so sweet and fair was she, with her yellow hair and her rosy cheeks. She could ride too, but not shoot. While Alan was practising with bow and arrow, she would be sewing her seam at her mother's knee, or watching the weaving, or learning from Oona how to twirl the flax for the spinning.

But all this time poor Oona is waiting with her story to tell!

"'Tis of a sweet young lassie," said the old woman, "as if it were sister to you, my bairn, but older, well on her way to be a woman; and ohon! and alas! Her mother dying when she was a wee bairn, and her father married again to the worst woman ever lived in this world. And this— Witch, for she was no better, put a cruel charm on the poor young thing, and turned her into a fiery snake, and bade her swim over the seas, and climb the Estmere Crags, and there bide.

"'And never, never shall ye be saved,' she said, 'till Kempion, the king's own son, come to the crag and thrice kiss thee. Till the world comes to an end, saved shall ye never be.' So the poor young thing, she took her yellow hair about her and tried to flee, but that moment the change came, and she turned into the most fearsome dragon beast that ever ye saw."

"I never will see one!" cried little Elspat, shivering and drawing close to her brother.

"I would," cried the Little Master, "if there was one alive now. I wish there was, so that I might kill it. Is there one, do ye think, Oona?"

"Nay! Nay, thank the good Lord!" the old nurse would say. "This was before good Saint Patrick of Ireland came and drove out all the wicked snakes and dragons and the like. But this poor thing, now, she wasn't wicked, ye see, for never the bit could she help herself. So there she stayed in a den, like, by the Estmere Crags, and all day long she cried on Kempion, if he would only come and save her. So word of that came to Kempion, the bravest prince that was in Scotland, and he built a boat, and he and his brother sailed the sea till they came near the Estmere Crags; and there they could not come anigh the shore, for the fiery beast that she was flung herself out of the den and struck the boat, and banged it as if she would have it in pieces. 'Be still!' the Prince bade her; but she cried all the louder, she never would quit her den till Kempion, the king's own son, would come to the crag and kiss her three times."

"Thrice, Oona!" cried the Little Master. "Not 'three times!'"

"Sure, child, dear, 'tis the same," the old nurse would say. "Thrice, then, it was. So with that what did he do, the bold lad that he was, but bend over the crag and kiss her on the ugly snout of her. Into her hole she swung, and out she came, and worse than before, all fire and flames; and what but the same words over again—she never would come out of it till Kempion, the king's own son, would come to the crag and kiss her thrice so, child, dear, that was what he did, the bold young heart of him, that's like your own, Master Alan. And with the third kiss, see now, what happened. All at once and behold, she changed from a flaming dragon to the most beautifulest maiden the sun ever shined on; and when he looked at her he saw—what would he see, Elspat, my bonnie?"

"His own true love!" cried little Elspat. "Oh, this is the part I like. It was his own true love, and her hair came down in a golden cloak to her feet that were white as cream. Go on, Oona!"

"And so it was!" said the old woman. "And ye may think how he grieved in his heart at the trouble that was put upon her. But now it was all past and gone, for he took the sweet young lady in his boat, his brother by to help him, and home they went to the king's court, and there Kempion married his own true love, and she to tread on velvet and lie on satin the rest of her life.

"So there is the story, and now run away to your supper, the two of ye."

"Good-by, Oona. Thank you for the story!" cried the Little Master. "Come, Elspat."

"By, Oona," said the little girl, throwing her arms around the nurse's neck. "Dear Oona!"

Then hand-in-hand the two children sped down the winding stone stair to the great hall, in a corner of which their little table was laid.

What did they have for supper? Porridge (they called it "parritch!") and milk—no sugar! and oatcake baked in the ashes. This was their supper and breakfast all the year round. They never thought of anything else. And for dinner—but we will tell about dinner another time. When they had finished their supper they would curl up together on the broad window-seat, and watch Duncan laying the table for my Lord's and my Lady's supper that was to follow; the plates and dishes of silver and pewter, the horn spoons (no forks in those days!), the gilt cup that the Queen had sent to my Lady on her marriage. Or they would gaze through the great window at the sunset sky with the dark trees against it, and the long sweep of the avenue; gaze eagerly till round the curve they saw the glitter of steel and heard the tramp of horses. Then down the long avenue, under the arching trees, would ride the Baron and his men, sometimes in hunting trim, with maybe a deer slung across the saddlebow of the chief huntsman, and each man of them dangling a rabbit or a brace of moorfowl; sometimes from war, grim and dusty, with dark stains on their leather coats and bright armor. When they saw this, little Elspat would cry, and shudder, and run to hide her head in her mother's lap; but Alan would throw his head back, and his eyes would flash and his hands clench. Was he not the Master of Morven, to be the Baron some far-off day? When he was a man he would ride with his father, on hunting, yes, and on war-parties too. But just then, most likely, Oona would come, blinking over her little horn lantern, and off must go little Master and little Lady to bed, as if they were any cottager's children instead of those of a noble Lord.

CHAPTER II

THE SMITH'S STORY. VALENTINE AND ORSON

IT was a wild afternoon of wind and rain, and the Little Master could not ride out to try the young hawks, as he had meant to do. Elspat was at her embroidery lesson, and Duncan would not let him play at ball in the great hall because he had broken a pane of glass there the day before. Glass was a rare thing in those days, and the pane might go long unmended. Altogether the Little Master was feeling rather forlorn; he looked out into the courtyard, where the rain was beating and the gusts whirling. Presently, from an open doorway came another kind of whirl, a puff of smoke shot through and through with fiery sparks; and at the same time, clink! clink! clink! came the friendly, musical chime of hammer on anvil. The Little Master's brow cleared; he would go see John, the smith. There would be warmth and light and friendliness. He ran down and across the court, and was soon there, shaking the raindrops from his doublet.

"And what are you doing, John Smith?" he asked.

The smith looked up with a friendly nod.

"You're there, Little Master, eh?" he said. "What am I doing? See! the sword my Lord broke on his last foray. 'Tis a good blade, and I shall make a rare dirk of it. Hey! Gibbie, blow me the bellows there!"

Gibbie, a rough, clumsy lad about Alan's own age, started forward, and in so doing jostled the Little Master, rubbing his sooty shoulder against the brown doublet.

"Out of my way, clumsy oaf!" cried the Little Master, and struck the lad a swinging blow on the ear. He drew back with a dark look.

"Hoot, toot!" said John, the smith. "Softly! softly! be not hard upon Orson, young Valentine! God made ye both with one stir of His finger in the clay-pool behind the door."

"I'm sorry, Gibbie," said Alan, who seldom could hold anger for a full minute. "I'll fight you if you like; or—here! Take this pastry cake! Cook gave it me out of the oven. Nay, you shall eat it!" and he thrust the dainty into the lad's mouth before he could speak. "There, John Smith, I have made amends. Now, show me the blade!"

The smith moved aside, and there on the anvil lay a broken sword—the hilt and perhaps half the blade— glowing ruddy white. Waves of light seemed to run up and down its length; Alan thought he had never seen so beautiful a thing. Now the smith struck the glowing metal lightly, and the sparks flew out like drops of fire on either side. Taking it up in his tongs, he looked it all over carefully, and shook his head.

"Not yet!" he said. "Into the fire with you once more, my beauty!"

He nodded to Gibbie, who blew the bellows with right good will, the Little Master lending a hand. The flames leaped roaring up the chimney, the coals glowed red and white. Thrusting the blade among them, he heaped them over it, turning it this way and that to meet the full strength of the fire; then drawing it out and laying it once more on the anvil, he fell to hammering and shaping the white-hot iron, humming to himself the while.

The two boys watched eagerly. Gibbie was to be a smith too when he was man grown, and then he would make swords and daggers for his young lord, and that would be Alan. Perhaps both were thinking the same thought; but now another came into Alan's mind.

"What were those names you called us but now, John Smith? Valentine, Orson? 'Tis a story, maybe. Tell it to us now! See, we are friends, aren't we, Gibbie?"

Gibbie nodded, his mouth full of pastry; John, the smith, looked across his anvil well pleased.

"'Tis a story, sure," he said, "a true tale my grandame

told me. Long ago she died, but I mind the most of it and you shall hear it."

He bent over his work again, turning and shaping the glowing blade, and as he wrought he told the story of Valentine and Orson.

"Once upon a day, and it was the day of Saint Valentine, the King of France rode out a-hunting with his knights. King Pepin it was. I mind me of the name, always thinking it strange to call a King so near after an apple. He hunted here and there in the forest, and as he looked through a green bush he saw something shining on the ground. He came nearer, and what was it but a new-born babe, wrapped in a mantle of gold that was pinned with a silver pin, and lying on a kerchief of scarlet silk. 'Twas a fair child, white as snow, with rose-red cheeks; and as the King looked it held out its arms and smiled like any cherub. So the King, who was kind of heart as any simple man, bade his knights take up the child and bring it home to court; and, since it was Saint Valentine's Day, he named the babe Valentine, and had him well and tenderly reared till he grew up a good knight and true. Now the very day that Valentine was made a knight came three pilgrims to the King making great outcry. There was a wild boy, they said, in Artois forest, who made destruction of everything that came within his reach, being strong as a bear, and savage as one: looked like a bear, too, they said, and altogether a fearsome thing. No one in that countryside dared go near him, and would King Pepin send help?

When Valentine heard that, he cried out for joy. 'Let me go, Master King,' he said, 'so I shall have my first knight's adventure!' So the King gave him his blessing and a good sword, which was worth three of it, and Sir Valentine mounted his horse and rode off to Artois forest. No sooner there but he saw the savage boy: a big, strong youth, of his own age or thereabout. He was shaggy as a bear, with the thick, brown hair that was on him, and for all his clothing a bear-skin over his shoulders, and in his hand a great, knotted club the size of my biggest sledge there." The smith nodded at a huge hammer that hung against the wall. "When the man-bear saw young Valentine he up with his club and at him with a growl and a roar as of twenty bears in one; but the knight was ready for him with his good blade, and I warrant you he roared in other fashion when he first felt cold steel."

"What like was the sword?" asked the Little Master. "Was it like the great two-handed one that hangs in the hall?"

"E'en just!" said John, the smith. "And you may guess how the taste of it came to him. Well, 'twas a stout battle, strength to skill, knotty oak to shiny steel, but it ended the right way, and the bear-lad came to court, who but he, tied to the tail of Sir Valentine's charger. At first he drooped and pined, but Valentine had that goodness and gentleness in him—mind that, my little Lord!—that he tamed the wild spirit of the lad till he had him like the dog that licked his hand, and taught him this and showed him that, till he grew a true and gentle squire to Valentine, and the two were like brothers for love.

"Now, there is half the story for you," said John Smith, "and for the other half ye must wait till I cool my blade in the water. Hey, there, Gibbie! shut thy mouth and open thine eyes, and fetch the bath!"

Gibbie ran, and brought from a dusky corner a long wooden box or trough, full of water. The smith held up the dagger, still glowing rosy white; then he plunged it into the cold water, and it hissed like the fiery snake in the old nurse's story. The brightness went out of it, and it lay black and lifeless.

"There!" said John Smith. "Lie there awhile, my beauty, and cool thy hot temper a bit. Finished, Master? Nay! nay! there's a mort of work yet before 'tis finished. This, look you, is to be as pretty a bit of steel as ever Lord wore at his belt. After this must come the oil bath, and then the rubbing down, and then the polishing, and then—whew! 'tis hot work enough, so it is!"

"Sit ye down and rest, John Smith!" cried Alan; "and while you rest, you can finish the story!" he added slyly. "You left it cut in the middle like an apple."

The smith rubbed his sooty hand across his forehead.

"The story!" he said. "'Tis more of supper than story I'm thinking now, Little Master. But you're right: a promise is a promise, full or fasting. Sit ye down again, and we'll have it. Where was I now? The work has driven the play clean out of my slow butter-wits."

"Valentine was grown up a knight!" said the Little Master.

"He had fought the wild boy!" said Gibbie.

"And made him tame, and was good to him!" said the Master.

"And his name was Orson!" both boys ended together.

"So 'twas!" said John the smith. "Meaning a bear, or some such, from his breeding and manners, though now he had left those behind.

"Well, sirs, so lived they happily at the King's court till one day some popinjay made game of Valentine for that he was a foundling and knew not his parents' name. Right mad was the young knight at that, and vowed he would not rest till he found those parents, were they living on earth. So to horse, and off he went, and Orson running beside him as fast as the steed could trot, his club over his shoulder.

"See now, lads, 'twould take the night to tell all these two saw and did; but at the last they came to a strange place. A great castle—"

"As big as this?" asked Alan.

"Four of this would not make it! And set in the middle of a lake, and leading to it a fair bridge, shining with silver and gold. Now who so glad as those two lads?

"But what happened? No sooner did they set foot on that fair bridge than out rang a peal of bells, full a hundred of 'em, that were hid under bridge where none might see them. With that the gate of the castle flew open and out came a giant, huge and grim."

"How big was he?" cried the boys.

"Oh, tall as a steeple and big as a hogshead! And he grinning with rage and brandishing a great mace set with steel spikes. He rushed at Valentine and he at him, and a great fight they had. Sparks flew like from my big sledge there when the iron is white-hot; and the giant roaring and yelling, and Valentine crying knightly words, no doubt, such as might fit.

"Ah, but lads, now the knight's good horse stumbled on a loose stone and fell with him, and at that the giant saw his chance and lifted his wicked mace to dash the lad's brains out. But even as he stooped down came a thundering blow on his own ugly head that sent him rolling on the ground, and over him stood faithful Orson with his club, and soon crushed the wicked life out of his body. Then those two lads gave thanks to Heaven as was meet: and loving thanks gave Valentine to his good brother, too, who stood by him so well. And then took the keys from the dead monster's girdle and so to search the castle.

"Well, sirs, as I said, the night would spend in the telling what they found there, of slain folk, and gold, and treasure without end; but at last, in a dark cell, who was there but a gentle lady, all forlorn with weeping and sorrow. Then who so kind as Valentine to dry her tears and lead her out into the sunlight, and when he had her comforted a bit, asked how she came there, and lo ye! the sad story of it!

"Seemed she was a Queen, and had known all joy and fortune, till one day a wicked ruffian slandered her to the King her husband, saying evil things of her; and he, foolish man (for Kings be but like other folk, lads!), believed the liar, and sent his own true sweet lady from his door. Weeping and wandering she went, hither and thither, till one day, in a deep, green woodland, two man-babes were born to her. The fairest babes in the world they were, she said, though one was rough with hair all over his body.

"But see what sorrow followed this poor dame! For, as she tended her babes there under the green trees, a bear rushed from the thicket and bore off the younger child in his jaws. The poor mother ran after as best she might, but swooned away from grief and weakness and lay long like one dead.

"'And better dead might I have been,' said that poor dame, 'for when I came to myself, my other babe, that I left wrapped in a scarlet kerchief on the ground, was gone, he also; nor from that woeful day have I ever seen either of my pretty babes again. Longing for death, I cared the less when this giant took me captive, and here in his castle I have lain ever since.'

"'But, lady,' said Valentine, 'would you know the scarlet kerchief that wrapped your babe?'

"With that he knelt on one knee and pulled forth the cloth in which himself had been found: lo, ye! it was the selfsame one, and Valentine had found his mother. Happy hour was that: and still happier when Valentine told the Lady Bellisance (for he knew her story at court, and she King Pepin's own dear sister!) that the villain who slandered her was dead, and in dying owned his crime of lying to her hurt. Then that sweet lady blessed God and embraced her newfound son.

"'But who is this hairy youth?' she asked; 'he much resembles thee. The bear devoured my younger babe, or sure that babe were he.'

"Then Valentine told how this lad was bred with bears, and found in their den.

"'Is there any mark,' he asked, 'by which you would know your son again?'

"'Ay!' she said; 'a crimson rose was stamped on his side.'

"'See, lady!' cried Valentine, 'here shines the mark today. My brother! oh, happy, happy day!'

"And happy day it was for the three of them, and happy years to follow, with joy and fortune and all good things. And in after times Valentine was King of France, and Orson King in his father's room, in Greece I mind it was. And here endeth the tale, and time, too, for a voice within me cries 'Kitchen!' louder than ever minstrel sang ballad. Away with ye, lads, and let me shut up my forge and home!"

CHAPTER III

THE *STEWARD'S STORY*. HYND HORN

THE great hall of the castle was a wonderful place to play in. It was so long that when you were at one end the other end looked dim and shadowy even by daylight, though to be sure this was partly because the windows were small and high up, and there were not many of them. There was not much furniture. The great oaken table stood at one end, with the straight-backed chairs around it, and at the head the Baron's great chair with the wolf's-heads carved on the arms. Then there was a high screen, covered with leather that had once been gilded, and a high-backed settle or two, and the huge sideboard or dresser where Duncan kept the platters and tankards of silver and pewter and the few bits of china, the Lady's posset-cup, and the flowered bowl from which little Elspat ate her bread and milk. And there was the enormous fireplace, with the black iron "dogs" and some wolf skins and deer skins in front of it; and that was all, except—a very important exception, the Little Master would have said—the banners and weapons and old armor that hung on the wall.

We will talk about those another time, but now I must say again that the hall was a wonderful place to play in. You could run races, and it did not take many turns to put Elspat quite out of breath. Or you could be robbers or dragons and live in the Darksome Dens at the farther end, away from the table and the fire, and rush out on the people who passed through. When you were dragons you threatened to devour them, but when you were robbers you just carried them to your secret hold and they had to tell a story by way of ransom. Most often it was Cripple Giles, the lame kitchen boy who helped Duncan sometimes; but he was not a very interesting captive, for he knew only one story, and that was very short. This was it:

> "Said the man to Sandy, Will ye lend me a mill?
> Said the man to Sandy, Will ye lend me a mill?
> Said the man to Sandy, "Will ye lend me a mill?"
> "Of course I will!" said Sandy.'
>
> "And Sandy lent the man a mill,
> And the man had the loan of Sandy's mill.
> "Will ye lend me a mill?" said Sandy;
> "Of course I will!" said the man."

Duncan was usually too busy to play or tell stories—that is, he never would be a captive in the Darksome Dens; but sometimes, if he felt very well (Duncan had rheumatism a good deal), he would be a besieged garrison behind the tall screen, and he made a fine one.

One day the children saw him sitting on his high stool beside the dresser, polishing the great silver grace-cup with a bit of soft leather, and humming to himself—it was always a good sign when Duncan hummed. The children looked at each other.

"Shall we?" whispered Elspat.

"Yes!" nodded the Little Master.

Down they went on hands and knees, and crept behind the great screen. It was wide as well as high, and they could creep along behind it till they were near the besieged garrison. The garrison sat all unconscious, polishing and humming, something with a refrain of:

"With a hey lillelu and a howlo lan!"

Suddenly a cry rang in his ears.

"Sound out, trumpets! up scaling ladders!"

In another minute the Little Master was on his knee, waving a flag, and Elspat had her arms around his neck, and both were crying:

"Yield! yield, or we put ye to the sword!"

"I yield me! I yield me!" cried the steward. "Have a care of the grace-cup, my Lord. Ye well-nigh knocked it out of my hand."

He set the cup carefully on the dresser and looked at it proudly.

"There's a polish, little Lady!" he said. "Like moon on the moat, no less. Yes! Yes! it takes a knack, d'ye see! it takes a knack."

"You are a prisoner!" shouted the Little Master, waving his flag.

"So I be; so I be!" said the steward. "A poor, doleful captive, to be sure. Shall we treat for ransom now, Sir Knight? There's a sweet cake in the cupboard here, and comfits in it."

"Sweet cake and story!" cried the children; "both, or no ransom, and the Darksome Dens for life."

"That were sair, indeed," said the steward. "'Tis a heavy ransom, but if must needs, then needs must. Sit ye down, the pair of ye, on the dresser here, for story or no story I must finish my polishing. Well, a-well! and what shall it be? Have ever I told ye the story of Hynd Horn?"

"Nay," said Elspat. "Ye spoke of it once, but got no further."

"Well, now shalt have it. 'Tis a bonny tale for lassies

and lads, too. Seems there was once a youth lived near the King's court—"

"What King?" the Little Master broke in.

"King Pepin of France?"

"Nay, nay!" said the steward. "No French frog-eaters, but a good King of bonny Scotland. As to just which one it was I misdoubt me, but maybe 'twas Malcolm Canmore[2], of whom they tell so many tales. However that be, there the lad lived, and there grew up, straight as a young tree, and well-nigh as tall. And he took service with the King, and all for the sake of his daughter Jean, that was fairer than the lily of the lake and white as that. But when the King found the love that was between the two an angry man was he. He banished young Hynd Horn from the court, and bade him go sail the salt seas over. Go he must and go he did, but before he sailed he saw his own true love once more, and she gave him a gay gold ring with three shining diamonds set therein.

"'So long as these stones shine bright and clear,' said the maiden, 'you'll know that all is well; but if they lose their color and their light then something has come between you and me.'"

With that they parted as fond lovers do, and Hynd Horn sailed away, and the maid stayed weeping at home.

2   Malcolm Canmore reigned, 1054-93, succeeding Macbeth.

Seven long years he journeyed hither and yon, now by sea and now by land, and often he looked on his ring to see if all was well with his true love, and always the diamonds shone up at him, only less bright than Lady Jean's eyes. But one day when he looked at his ring the stones had no light for him, but hung all cold and dead in their ring of gold. Then Hynd Horn said: "Woe is me! Some ill has befallen." And he hoisted his brown sails and away home to his own country.

Come to land, the first he met was an old beggar-man, and he asked him for the news: "'For,' says he, ''tis seven long years since I've seen this land.'"

"'There's no news,'" said the old beggar-man, "'or only such a scrap as I could put in my pouch, and that's that our King's only daughter is to be married to-day.'"

"Now," said Hynd Horn, "give me your beggar's coat, and I'll give you my scarlet cloak instead; and give me your old pike-staff and hat, and you shall be right well paid for that."

The old man wondered more than a little, but surely he asked no better, and in short space he was off to the mill—who but he—in a fine scarlet cloak, with white silver in his pouch, and Hynd Horn was away to the King's palace dressed in the beggar's rags, with his old hat pulled down over his brows. No one might know him, even were it not for the long years since he had come there. He knocked at the gate, and when the porter asked what he came seeking he said: "I ask a drink for the sake of young Hynd Horn."

Now that word came to the bonny bride where she sat in her bower, sad at heart; and when she heard the name of Hynd Horn, she rose up in her satin gown, with the gold combs in her hair, and took a golden cup in her hand and came tripping down the stair.

She looked kindly on the beggar-man and held out the cup: "For anyone who asks in that name," she said, "shall gain what he seeks."

He drank from the cup, and then into it he dropped the ring and gave it back to the lady. When she saw that, she cried out, and her hand went to her heart:

> "Oh! got ye this by sea or by land,
> Or got ye it off a dead man's hand?"

For they had told her, d'ye see, little Lord and Lady, that her lover was cold and dead. And he said, as the song tells it:

> "I got it not by sea nor by land,
> Nor got I it off a dead man's hand;
> But I got it at my wooing gay,

And I give it to you on your wedding-day."

Oh! but who then so glad as Lady Jean?

"I'll cast away my satin gown,"

she cried,

> "And follow you from town to town;
> And I'll take the gold combs from my hair,
> And follow you forever mair."

With that the beggar let fall his cloak, and there stood young Hynd Horn, and shone like a Prince with gold and jewels; and all that saw them cried out 'twas shame and sorrow that ever such fair and true lovers should have been parted. And so there was a wedding indeed that day, but young Hynd Horn was the bridegroom, and what became of the other the song says naught of, nor did I ever care.

"Now, little Lord and Lady, there is your story, and have I paid my ransom well?"

WITH THAT THE BEGGAR LET FALL HIS CLOAK, AND THERE
STOOD YOUNG HYND HORN.

CHAPTER IV

ELSPAT'S STORY. THE JOLLY GOSHAWK

"DONALD," said little Elspat, "is that a goshawk?"

"A goshawk it is, my little lady," said Donald the falconer, stroking the bird that was perched on his wrist; "and as fine a one as is in Scotland this day. Look at the beauty of him; see how he holds his head up. That's for pride, d'ye see. The goshawk is a proud bird; like a lord among birds he is, as it might be my Lord your father."

"Is he jolly?" asked the little girl.

"Jolly?" repeated Donald. "I don't rightly know whether he is jolly or not, little lady; but his crop is full of good corn, and he knows he is going out for sport soon to the green wood. Yes, yes! Jolly enough he will be, I'm thinking."

"Why don't you ask him?" said Elspat. "Cannot all goshawks speak?"

"Never a one that e'er I met with, my Lady!" said the falconer, with a puzzled look. "What notion is in your pretty head now? Parrots speak, and the like outlandish birds; but a good Scottish hawk—nay! nay! he has other work to do than talking, that is only good for chattering mortals."

"I know what she means!" said the Little Master, who was standing by one of the perches, feeding a splendid falcon, who shook his smooth plumage and clawed the boy's sleeve for pleasure as he snatched one morsel after another from his hand. "She is thinking of the Goshawk ballad that Mother sang us last even. That is not true, Elspat. 'Tis only an old story, like all the ballads."

"Nay! but some of them are true, Alan!" cried the little girl; "true as true, for Mother said so."

"Oh! yes, the fighting ballads," said the boy; "they are true enough; but this kind is—well, it's different. 'Tis next neighbor to a fairy story, child."

"'Tis pretty all the same," said Elspat, "and ye need not be calling me child, Alan, that are none so very old yourself. Would you like to hear it, Donald?" she asked wistfully.

"Deed and I would, then!" said the falconer, heartily. "Any tale that you told would be good to hear, my little lady-lass; and when 'tis about a hawk, ye see, why—'tis as it were made for me, d'ye see? And who knows but the birds themselves will be pleased?" he added, stroking his favorite again. "Listen now, Lightning; hear to the little lady!"

The hawk gave a short scream, and clawed Donald's hand.

"Go on! he says," said the falconer. "He's hungry for it."

"Well!" said Elspat. "It was a young knight, was parted from his true maiden; mostly they all do be!" she added, a little sadly. "And he called his jolly goshawk, and told him 'twas well he could speak and flee, for he must take a message to his true love from him.

"'But how will I know her?' asked the hawk, 'when I never set eyes on her?' So he told him, four and twenty ladies would be coming home from the mass, and well he would know his true-love, the fairest lady there. So off the bird flew, and came to the castle, and lighted on the ash tree, and sang a song about their love, the knight's and the lady's. So when the sweet lady heard that, she came to the window, and the goshawk threw her the letter he had brought in his beak all the way. And he said she was to send her lover a send, for he had sent her two; and tell him where he might see her soon, or he could not live.

"Then the lady said; wait now, till I mind the words! She said:

> 'I send him the ring frae my finger,
>   The garland frae my hair;

> I send him the heart from out my breast,
> What would my love have mair?
> And at the fourth kirk in fair Scotland
> Ye'll bid him wait for me there.'

"Then the goshawk flew back, and the lady went to her father and asked would he give her what she would ask for. And he said, never beg him for that Scottish knight, for never more should she see him.

"Nay," she said, "but just an asking; that if she died in fair England, he would take her to Scotland to be buried. At the first church in Scotland they should let all the bells be rung; at the second church they should sing hymns and prayers for her; at the third church they should deal gold for her sake; and at the fourth church they should bury her. Is that right, Alan?"

"Right enough," said the Little Master. "But the best part is to come."

"I know! I know!" cried Elspat. "Her father said yes, she might have that asking, but why did she talk so, when she wasna going to die? And then she went to her chamber, and she took a sleepy draught, and she fell down all pale and cold as any corpse. 'She's dead!' said her mother. But the old witch-wife said, 'Maybe ay and maybe no! But drop the hot lead on her cheek, and drop it on her chin, and drop it on her bosom white, and she'll maybe speak again.' For she knew about her true love, ye see, Donald, and she said 'twas much a young lady would do, to win to her true love. So they did that, cruel that they were; but she never stirred nor spake, so they thought she was dead indeed, and they made her a gown of satin and a coffin of cedar with silver edges; and they started with the funeral train for bonny Scotland. But now, ye see, Donald, the goshawk had told his master all she bade him; and when the funeral train came to the fourth church in bonny Scotland, there was the knight with all his merry young men, waiting for them. And he bade them set down the bier, till he should look on her; for the last time he saw her, she was bright as a rose, he said. So then he stripped the sheet down from her face, and—oh, Donald! what think you? The lady opened her eyes and looked full at him. And 'Oh!' she said, 'give me a piece of your bread, love, and let me drink of your cup, for long I have fasted for your sake.' And she bade her seven brothers, that brought her there, go home again and blow their horns. And she said, she did not come to bonny Scotland to lie down in the clay, but she came to wear the silks so gay; nor came she among the dead to rest, but she came to bonny Scotland to the man that she loved best. And that is the end, Donald; and is it not a bonny story? And do ye think Lightning understood it?"

"And if he did not," said Donald, "he is not the hawk I take him for."

CHAPTER V

ALAN'S STORY. COO-MY-DOO

"DON'T ye think maybe it might be true, Alan, about the goshawk? Don't ye think Lightning could speak to us if he only would?"

"I don't think it," said the Little Master. "I have tried to make him, often and often, but he will never say a word. I think it's only a story like Coo-my-doo."

"Tell me Coo-my-doo!" cried little Elspat. "Is't a new tale? Did Donald tell ye?"

"Ay!" said the Little Master. "Yesterday it was, out in the forest. We sat under the great oak to eat our dinner, and Donald told me the tale. If I tell it now will you mend my net, Elsie?"

"Indeed and I will!" cried the little girl. "I'd mend it without a story, Alan, but I'd like it fine with one."

Out came her housewife, a pretty red leather case with silver edges that the Baron had brought her from the great city; down she sat on her own little stool in the corner of the great fireplace, slipped on her tiny thimble and took up the broken net and set busily to work. The

Little Master, nodding his thanks, stretched himself at full length on the white bearskins, and kicked his heels thoughtfully in the air.

"It was thinking of the Jolly Goshawk," he said, "made Donald call this tale to mind. Once upon a time Earl Mar's daughter was playing under an oak tree, and she saw a fair white doo sitting on a branch."

"Mother says 'tis 'dove' in the English!" said little Elspat.

"Maybe so," replied the Little Master. "But 'tis doo' in Scots and this is a Scots tale. 'So,' says she to the doo,

> 'Oh, Coo-my-doo, my Love so true,
>   If ye'll come down to me
> Ye'll have a cage of good red gold,
>   Instead of simple tree.'

No sooner had she said the words than down flew the doo and lighted on her head and cooed sweetly. So she took him home to her bower and petted him and gave him sweets and made much of him; and he ate from her hand, and cooed, and shook his white wings, and no one ever saw so fair a bird. But when the sun set, all of a sudden he changed from a bird into a beautiful prince dressed in white velvet and gold. The lady was sore surprised at that, and asked him who he was and where he came from, and he said he had just flown across the sea that very day. 'My mother is a queen,' he said, 'and she knows magic, too; she turned me into a doo, so that I could fly about wherever I liked, but now that I have seen you I don't want to fly any more.'

Then the lady said: 'Oh, Coo-my-doo, my Love so true, you must never leave me.'

And he said he wouldn't, and so he stayed with her and they were very happy, and nobody knew anything about it, for whenever anyone was coming he turned back into a doo, you see.

Well, but after a long time there came along a lord of high renown and wanted to marry her, and brought her fine presents."

"What kind of presents?" asked Elspat.

"Oh, I don't know! Gold combs, I suppose, and other woman's gear!" said the Little Master, rather loftily. "But she said no, she didn't want them or him either, and she would rather stay at home with her bird, Coo-my-doo. Then Earl Mar was very angry, and he said:

> 'To-morrow, ere I eat or drink,
> That bird I'll surely kill.'

But Coo-my-doo was sitting in his golden cage and heard what he said.

'Tis time I was away!' said he. So off he flew, over the sea and far away till he came to his mother's castle. It had gold towers, and he lighted on one and his mother saw him.

> 'Get dancers for to dance,' she said,
> 'And minstrels for to play,
> For here's my dear son Florentine
> Come back with me to stay.'

But he told her he wanted neither dancers nor minstrels; he wanted twenty-four strong men turned into storks, and his seven sons into swans, and himself into a gay goshawk.

The Queen said that was pretty hard work, but she would try, and so she did, and soon she had them all turned, and off they flew over the sea again with Coo-my-doo—only now he was a goshawk, you know—at their head.

They got back to Earl Mar's castle only just in time, for he was going to make his daughter marry the lord whether she would or no, and though she wept sore, he said she must. So the wedding party was all ready and just coming out of the castle to go to the church, when a great rustling sound was heard overhead. Everybody looked up, and there was a goshawk flying like the wind, and behind him seven swans, and behind them twenty-four great gray storks. Nobody had ever seen such a sight, and they all stared with their mouths open, but before they had time to shut them, down flew the birds right among them! The storks seized the strong men and held them tight, so that they could not move; the swans caught the bridegroom and tied him fast to a tree; while the goshawk lighted on the bride's shoulder and whispered in her ear, and the next moment came the swans and whirled round her and caught her up in the air; the goshawk led the way, the storks followed, and away they all flew over the sea to his kingdom and never were seen again.

The wedding people stared and stared, and rubbed their eyes, and thought they must be dreaming; but Donald ended it like this, out of the old ballad:

> 'Naething could the company do,
> And naething could they say;
> But they saw a flock of pretty birds
> That took their bride away.'"

CHAPTER VI

THE LADY'S STORY. TAMLANE

"MOTHER," said little Elspat, "if I should go to the greenwood would Tamlane be there?"

The Lady of the Castle looked up from her embroidery. "Tamlane!" she repeated. "What has put Tamlane into my lassie's head?"

"Oona was telling me about him," said Elspat timidly.

"Oona had little to do, filling your head with a parcel of old tales!" said the Lady gravely; but the next moment she looked up, and meeting the child's wondering eyes, a smile broke over her sweet face.

"But truth to tell, lassie," she added, "when I was your age I would often be thinking of young Tamlane myself."

"Who is young Tamlane, Mother?" cried the Little Master, who came running in at this moment, with a great deerhound puppy gamboling at his heels. "Down, Wallace! Down, I tell thee. Is Tamlane a lad, Mother?"

"Oh! Alan," cried Elspat; "'tis the bonniest tale of all! Tell him, Mother, will you? Ah! do now, sweet, my dear!"

"Do, Mother!" echoed the boy. "You are aye telling Elspat tales; I never hear the half of them."

"If you were a douce lassie, instead of a hilty-skilty laddie," said the Lady, "you would hear them all, Alan. Would you like to learn to sew your seam and do your broidery, like a lassie, eh?"

"Indeed, no!" cried the boy, tossing his head scornfully. "I wouldna be a lassie for all—"

"Alan, Mother was a lassie one time!" said little Elspat.

"And Father was a laddie," said the Lady, smiling; "and Tamlane—Well, sit ye down, Alan, and you shall hear who Tamlane was.

"'Tis an old, old story, and it begins telling how Fair Janet sat in her bower alone, sewing her milk-white seam, when there came a longing on her for the sweet greenwood."

"Ah!" said Elspat with a sigh. "Often have I felt that same, Mother dear."

"And often do you go, little one, but not alone, as Janet went. For she let fall her seam, and away to Carterhaugh, that was a deep forest hard by her father's hall. When she came there she began to pull the wildflowers; when up from behind a bush started young Tamlane, the fairy knight, and he all in fairy green, with gold about his neck and a bright star on his brow. At first he chid her for pulling the flowers; but when he saw how fair she was he spoke sweetly to her, and his voice was like running water. 'Tis long to tell, children, but between this and that, these two, Fair Janet and the fairy knight, became lovers true and dear. But there was a trouble at Janet's heart, and she asked the young knight had he ever been christened in God's name. He told her yes, he was a knight's and a lady's son, and as well christened as she herself.

"But," he said, "three years ago a strange chance came to me. I rode out a-hunting one day, and as I rode over yon high hill there blew upon me a drowsy, drowsy wind, so that my eyes closed for all I could do, and I fell from my horse in a dead sleep. It was the Queen of Fairies sent that wind, Janet; she took me away to Fairyland, and there I have lived ever since. But to-morrow night is Hallowe'en, when the Fairy Court rides through the land, and you can rescue me if you will. At midnight, go and stand by Miles Cross, and make a circle with holy water. Then by will come the fairies, three bands of them. The first band that rides by, take no heed of them. The second band that rides by, salute them reverently. The third band that rides by is clad in robes of green, and that is the head court of all, and in it rides the Queen, and I upon a milk-white steed, with a bright star in my crown. Pull me from my horse,

"Up From Behind A Bush Started Youn Tamlane."

Janet, and hold me tight, whatever happens. Whatever shape I take, whatever pain you feel, hold me fast, for if you loose your hold I am lost forever."

At midnight Fair Janet stood by the lonesome Miles Cross in the wild heather. She cast a circle with holy water, and soon she saw the Fairy Court come riding over the hill, with golden bells ringing and sweet voices singing, more sweet than any on earth:

> "By then gaed the black, black steed,
>   And by then gaed the brown;
> But Janet has gripped the milk-white steed
>   And pulled the rider down."

Then there went up a strange, eerie cry, "Tamlane, he's awa'!" and all in a moment the Fairy Court was gone, and nought to be seen save what Janet had in her arms. But oh! children, what was it that she held? It turned cold, cold like ice on a frozen lake. Janet felt the very heart freezing in her, but she held fast. Then all in a moment it changed to a fire, and the flames leaped up about her, and she felt her flesh scorching in bitter pain; but still she held fast, like the faithful maid she was. Again it changed, and now in her arms was a great serpent, that coiled and twisted round her, and hissed in her face with open jaws; but Janet gripped the smooth coils hard, and looked steadily into the glittering eyes; and again a change came, and now she held a great white swan, that struck at her with its hard beak, and shook its strong wings, and strove with all its might to fly away. But love was stronger than all, children; though Janet was well-nigh dead with pain and fright, still she held fast, and lo ye! now in a moment all was over, and there in her arms lay young Tamlane, her own true love. She cast her green mantle over him, and from that moment he was safe, and no fairy charm could touch him more.

"And so the story ends, children dear—"

"But tell what the Queen said, Mother," cried Elspat. "Oh, tell Alan that!"

> Out then and spake the Queen of Fairies,
> Out of a bush of broom:
> "She that has rescued young Tamlane
> Has gotten a stately groom."
> Out then and spoke the Queen of Fairies,
> Out of a bush o' rye,
> "She's ta'en away the bonniest knight
> In all my companie."

"That is all I mind of it, lassie. Now off to your play, the two of you, and if you find Tamlane in the greenwood be sure you bring him to me!"

CHAPTER VII

THE FALCONER'S STORY. THE BONNIE MILLDAMS OF BINNORIE

"OH! Alan—I mean Tamlane!" cried Fair Janet. "I canna hold ye if ye wriggle so hard. Bide a bit, till I get my breath again."

"Ho!" cried the Fairy Knight. "I must wriggle. I am a serpent, and if you let me go, Janet, I shall be lost forever, you know. Hold on tight; I shall turn into a fire in a minute."

Poor Janet held on as tight as she could, panting and crimson; the serpent wriggled and hissed frightfully.

"I'm frightened!" cried the maiden at last. "You look fearsome, Tamlane. Is it near done?"

"Almost!" hissed Tamlane. "Now I am a fire. Do I burn you?"

"Yes!" faltered Janet. "You burn me fine, but it's not so bad as the serpent part."

"Now I am a swan!" the knight announced. "I am afraid I must hurt you a bit, my beak is so hard; but this is the last, you know, Janet, and then you'll only have to throw your green mantle over me, and—"

"What is to do here?" said a voice behind them. "What is to do here, Master?"

The knight started, and turning, saw Donald, the falconer, looking sternly down upon him.

"Striking a lassie!" the old man went on. "And your own sister, too. That is a sight I never thought to see from my Lord's son."

"Oh! Donald, he wasn't! He wasn't!" cried little Elspat eagerly. "He is Tamlane, and—oh, wait; wait a minute—there!"

She snatched up her little mantle and threw it over her brother, who stood silent and shamefaced. "Now he is safe, and the Fairy Queen canna touch him more; do ye see, Donald?"

"Tamlane?" said the falconer doubtfully.

"Ay, sure; 'tis a fairy tale. Mother told it to us, and we made a play of it. He was a fairy knight, and I was Fair Janet, and he had to turn into a fire and a snake and all the other things, else I never could have got him free. 'Tis a bonny play, Donald!"

"Maybe so," said Donald. "It looked a bit rough, as between a knight and a lady; but play is play, and I'll say no more. Now sit ye down, lad and lass, and see what Joan cook has sent you for a noon-piece."

The Little Master cast the green mantle aside and sprang up with a joyful shout, and Elspie clapped her hands for joy. "'Tis a doo-pasty!" she cried. "Oh, Alan, 'tis a doo-pasty!"

The "doo-pasty," which was neither more nor less than a pigeon pie, was set on the grass, and soon the children were enjoying themselves to the full. It was a lovely spot they had chosen for their play; a little open glade in the forest, where the short grass was flecked with sunshine, and shaded by the spreading branches of a great ash tree.

They did not know that they were having a picnic, for they had never heard the word. They had just had leave to come to the forest with Donald, and have their noon-piece there, and that over, Donald was to tell them a story. They reminded him of this when nothing was left of the pasty save the crumbs, which Elspat scattered for the birds.

"A tale?" said Donald, stretching himself on the grass, and looking up into the great green tent above him. "You bairns are aye wanting tales. Hark to the mavis yonder! He tells a sweeter tale than ever old Donald could. And yet that was a sweet tale I heard last night," he added. "David sang it to his harp; maybe you heard it; the song of the Two Sisters of Binnorie? Nay?" "Then I will—nay, I cannot sing it; yonder old corby could sing better than I; I'll tell it in plain words as well as I can.

"'Twas of two fair sisters and a gallant knight that came a-wooing. It began like this, I mind me:

> 'There were two sisters sat in a bower,
> Binnorie, O Binnorie!
> A knight came there, a noble wooer,
> By the bonny mill-dams o' Binnorie.
>
> He courted the eldest wi' glove and ring,
> Binnorie, O Binnorie!
> But he loved the youngest above all thing,
> By the bonny mill-dams o' Binnorie.'

And why he should court the elder one when 'twas the other he loved passes old Donald's wit to tell ye, bairns; but so it was, and the elder hated her sister therefor.

"One day she called her and said: 'Come away down to the river strand with me!' The maid came, thinking no harm, and as she stood on a stone, what does that wicked other one do but push her into the deep, swift-flowing water! Oh? but the poor young maid cried on her:

> 'O sister, sister, reach your hand,
> And you shall be heir of half my land!'

"And again:

> 'O sister, reach me but your glove,
> And Sweet William shall be your love!'

"But that wicked one stood by and saw the poor maid borne down the stream, and never spoke nor reached her hand."

"So down she came to the mill-dam—"

"The wicked one?" asked Elspat.

"Nay, nay, lassie! The other, to be sure, that was floating in the water; and the miller's son saw her and called to his father, here was either a mermaid or a swan. The miller drew the water out and there he found the poor sweet lassie, but cold and dead was she, and yet fairer than any lily. Round her middle was a girdle of pure gold, and strings of pearls in her yellow hair, and her white fingers set with jewel rings.

"By then came a harper, one like our David, that went from hall to hall playing and singing, and when he saw that piteous sight he made a great moan and sighed and wept. Then he took three locks of her yellow hair and strung his harp with them, and then he took his way to her father's hall that he knew well. They were all sitting round the board—the lord her father and the lady her mother, and that wicked maiden her sister—and she all clad in her silks and velvets, and thinking now she would win Sweet William's heart for sure; but he, poor lad, looked ever over his shoulder at the door, wondering why his true love was so long a-coming. But instead of her, in came the harper and sat down among them and took up his harp to play. But oh, bairns, when he did that a strange marvel befell, for the harp spoke and sang with its own voice, and never a word from him. And—but see now! the words are so bonny. I must mind them if I can, for my own words are poor beside them. David sang, then:

> And soon the harp sang loud and clear,
>   Binnorie, O Binnorie!
> 'Farewell, my father and mother dear!'
>   By the bonny mill-dams o' Binnorie.
>
> And next when the harp began to sing,
>   Binnorie, O Binnorie!
> 'Twas Farewell, sweetheart!' said the string,
>   By the bonny mill-dams o' Binnorie.
>
> And then as plain as plain could be,
>   Binnorie, O Binnorie!
> 'There sits my sister who drowned me!'
>   By the bonny mill-dams o' Binnorie."

CHAPTER VIII

THE DAIRYMAID'S STORY.
LEEZIE LINDSAY

IT was was so hot that the children had taken refuge
the dairy, the coolest place in the whole castle. This was
a great stone-vaulted room, with small windows that let
in little light; however hot the sun might glare outside,
inside there was always a dim, cool twilight, with the
milk glimmering in its great pans of polished stone, and
the pleasant, cool smell of buttermilk and cheese filling
the air. So here, on this burning July morning, were the
Little Master and Elspat, curled up comfortably on a great
stone table, watching Leezie, the dairymaid, making
up her butter. Some of it she made into little pats, and
stamped them with the thistle stamp which was Elspat's
great admiration; some of it she made into great, smooth
rolls; and all of it was yellow as gold and sweet as clover.

"Is your name Lindsay, Leezie?" asked little Elspat, after
watching this delightful process in silence for some time.

"No, my leddy lassie!" said Leezie. "My name is Cameron. Why?"

"You were singing a song about Leezie Lindsay," said the child. "Sing it again, will ye no?"

"Deed I'll not!" said Leezie good-naturedly. "I'm hoarse as a corby now, wi' singing all the morning, lassie. I canna bring my butter without singing, however it is."

"Tell it, then!" said Elspat. "Alan would like fine to hear it; wouldn't ye, Alan?"

"I would that!" said Alan.

"You bairns are aye for singing and telling," said Leezie. "Weel, then, 'tis an old song that, and Leezie Lindsay was a young leddy, and a fair one, and lived in Edinbro' town, so she did. And there came a lad wooing her, and asked her would she go to the Hielands wi' him? But the leddy shook her head and said how could that be, when she did not know his name, nor the place where he would be going? So he said she would find out soon, and his name was Ronald, and he loved her weel. So she put on her coats o' green satin, and off she went with the lad. Oh, but it was a weary way, bairns; and long before night poor Leddy Leezie was so done that she scarce could put foot before toe, as the saying is. But at long last they came to a poor bit cottage, and an old woman by it; and when the old body saw the lad she began to cry out and make a great stir; but he said a word in her ear, and then he turned to Leezie. "'This is my mother, bonny Leezie,' he said; 'now, mother, give us our supper, for we have traveled long and far.'

"With that the old body set out curds and whey for them, and made a bed of green rushes on the floor, and there Leddy Leezie must sleep, and think of her grand bed at home. Sair was her heart, and sair she mourned her folly; but when the lad roused her in the morning, and bade her go milk the goats and kye[3], she wept salt tears, and said with many a sigh:

'The leddies of Edinbro' City,
    They milk neither goats nor kye!'

"But he bade her be blithe, and he would show her fine things yet; so the poor lassie e'en made the best of it, and a poor best it's like it was, and worse for the dumb creatures than for her, I'm saying. But when they had had their curds and whey again, and maybe a bit of bannock with it, though the song says nought of that, the lad said they must on again, for there was more to show her before another night came on. So poor Leezie must take her weary steps again, and like to fall she was upon the way, and sighing and moaning; little courage she had, if the song tells right. I never thought mickle of city lasses myself.

3   Kye=cows

"Weel, and to tell all, they came at last to a fair great castle, the like of it was not in Scotland for bigness; and when they came to the great door, what would they see but it opening, and an old lady coming to meet them, was dressed like a Queen, and the keys of all the castle in her hand. "'You're welcome home, Lord Ronald, my son!' she said; 'and your bonny bride is welcome, too. Here are the keys, bonny Leezie,' she said, 'take them, for all is at your command.'

"Ye see, bairns, all the time it was Lord Ronald McDonald, a chieftain o' high degree; and he fooling the lassie that was his own true love, and I never liked him for that; but, however it was, now she was a great leddy, and she needna eat curds and whey unless she liked them. I know who likes them weel enough, and ye shall have some when my butter is done; but one thing I'll tell ye, bairns: if Jamie, the cook-lad, played me a trick like that, it's no wife he'd get, but the hard side o' my butter-paddle over his head."

CHAPTER IX

THE TRUE STORY BEGINS

DID I say that the dairy was the coolest place in the castle? Nay! there was one cooler. Under the lowest story, dug deep in the living rock of the foundations, were chambers cool enough in the hottest day of midsummer, for no ray of sunlight ever entered them. These were dungeons, such as were to be found in all the old castles of those days. Little Elspat had never been in them; she never passed that side of the wall without a shudder; they were empty, but they had not always been so. Alan could remember, when he was very little, hearing groans and cries issuing from the narrow slits which served for windows in those gloomy vaults. He had asked what the sounds meant, and his mother had wept, and his father sternly bade him hold his peace and go to his play. Once, too— but this was long after, when he was quite a big boy— a huntsman had been put in one of the dungeons for a day or two, as a punishment for forgetting the hawks' messes. He was a young fellow whom Alan knew well. It was dreadful to think of his being shut up in that gloomy place while all the rest were shouting and playing in the sunlight. When Duncan went down to take him his poor supper, Alan stole down the stone stair behind him, and peeped into the prison. The air was cold, damp and mouldy; it struck a chill to his heart, and he cried out pitifully, and begged Duncan to let Sandy out, and he would feed the hawks himself for a week; but Duncan was angry, and threatened to tell the Baron if he stayed a moment longer; that sent him flying back up the stairs, with only a word cried to poor Sandy, to take heart and the days would soon pass. So they did, and Sandy never forgot the kindness, and would have given his life for the Little Master.

One day— in August it was, when the hay harvest was being gathered, and all hands in the castle were busy enough with peaceful tasks— a horseman came spurring up the avenue in hot haste. His buff coat was spattered with mud; his horse was covered with sweat and foam; it was plain that he had ridden fast and far.

Alan was just coming out of the door, and the stranger hailed him, in a voice hoarse and broken with fatigue.

"Ha! lad, these to your Lord, in haste!"

As he spoke, he threw himself from his horse, and held out a letter, sealed with a great red seal.

"In haste!" he repeated. "And say where my horse

may be cared for, for I must mount and ride again so soon as may be."

Others had heard the galloping hoofs, and now Tam the horseboy came running to take the weary horse, and Duncan the steward greeted the horseman, and bade him come in and take rest and refreshment. Meantime Alan ran to the inner courtyard, where he knew his father was overseeing the training of the young hawks. Holding out the packet, he told briefly of the coming of the messenger, and the need of haste.

The Baron took the letter and turned it over, frowning at it.

"What is here?" he asked. "Know'st thou the man?"

"Nay, my Lord; he is a stranger; but he saith 'haste, haste;' and he hath ridden fast and far, as his horse and himself both show."

"Here is a to-do!" muttered the great Lord, still frowning at the packet. He broke the seal, and stared at the contents, frowning still more heavily.

"Priest's gear!" he muttered to himself. Then aloud: "Bid Father Neil come hither!"

"So please you, my Lord, Father Neil is away; he went to the Dowie Glen this morning, to comfort a dying man."

The Baron swore at the priest and at the dying man.

"Here is a to-do!" he repeated. "Ever in the way when you want them not, out of the way when need is of them. Is there anyone else can make out these scratches, think you?"

Alan blushed fiery red, and hung his head. "I—I—" he stammered, "if it please you, father, it may be that I could read them, or some of them at least."

"Thou!" said the Baron. "What hast thou to do with such gear?"

"I—I pray you forgive me, father! 'Twas a scroll that Father Neil had cast aside. He said I might have it; and—on rainy days I have studied it whiles, and—I thought maybe, an you were fain to know—"

"Pshaw!" growled the Baron. "Would he make a priest of thee, like Gavin Douglas? Were it any other day but this, I would thrash thee soundly, and crop the ears of him who taught thee against my will; but as this gear stands—have thy way, lad! Here! see an thou canst make out what is toward."

With trembling hands the boy took the scroll, and slowly, and with many a slip and stumble, read aloud:

"To the good Lord of Morven, these in haste.

I ride into England to take a pray, with me Graeme and Lindsay, Gordon and menny more. Wherefor mount and ride, thou and thine, with speed, with speed. The meeting place is Green Leyton, down over Ottercap Hill.

So greets thee in felos hyppe
James of Douglas."

Looking up, Alan saw his father still frowning heavily, and pulling his great beard, as he did when he was angry.

"Please you, Lord father," said the boy, "be not angry with Father Neil, for indeed and truly, my reading is no fault of his, but mine own. I saw him read, and longed to know what was in the scroll; and so I watched and listened, unbeknown to him, and—"

The Baron started and turned to him.

"Prut!" he said. "I was not thinking of thy pribbles and prabbles, boy. Time enough for thee to forget priest's knowledge, when thou ridest the Border with me; for this once, it was well enough that someone could read the Douglas his summons. Behooves us mount and ride, and no more about scrawling and scrivelling."

He strode out of the courtyard, calling to his people. In another moment all was bustle and confusion. Men ran hither and thither, calling and shouting. Armor was taken down from the walls and hastily buckled on, without stay for the customary polishing which was the pride of the old men-at-arms. Horses were fed and groomed (they must be in good condition, however it fared with their riders), wallets were stuffed with provisions and hung at saddlebows. All the time the Baron strode hither and thither, giving orders, helping on this work with a word of cheer, and that with a cuff or a curse. In a wonderfully short space of time the troop was equipped and mounted, and rode away down the avenue, shouting and singing.

Poor Alan! When the Baron spoke of his riding the Border with him, the boy thought for a moment that he was to go on this foray; but after that brief word his father took no note of him. The Lady came downstairs, pale and anxious, little Elspat beside her. Her the Baron kissed and embraced, bidding her be of good cheer, all would be well. He tossed the little girl up in his arms, and laughed to see her golden curls fly up around her rosy face; but for Alan he had neither word nor look, and the boy's heart beat fast with disappointment and mortification. But at the last, when Lord Morven had swung himself into the saddle, Brown Bess already pawing and prancing with eagerness to be off, he turned for a moment and looked at the boy.

"Master of Morven," he said, "look you to the castle and the women! I leave them in your hands."

With that he laughed and rode away; and Alan knew not whether his heart were more cast down or lifted up.

Three days passed, and never a sign of the Baron or his men. The lady wept and trembled over her embroidery frame, for she hated the Border forays for the wild and cruel things they were. Alan and Elspat tried to cheer and comfort her, bringing her flowers and berries from the fields, and trying to turn her thoughts by begging for song or ballad, such as they loved best to hear in her sweet voice; but she could not sing, the Lady said.

"Then I will sing to you!" cried little Elspat. And she sang the song of Glenlogie and his true love, how they were parted, and how the maiden drooped and fainted till her own good knight came to cheer her up. Just as she was singing the last words:

"Oh binna feared, mither, I'll maybe no dee!"

Alan cried, "Look! who is it coming down the road?"

Three horsemen were coming, riding slowly down the broad avenue. Two of them were soon recognized as Black Rob and Walter of Welthorpe, two of the Baron's men-at-arms who had ridden away with him three days before; but who was the third?

Alan looked eagerly, but there was no familiar look about the bent head and bowed shoulders; soon he saw that the stranger's arms were tied behind his back, and his feet securely fastened under the horse. A prisoner!

"WITH THAT HE LAUGHED AND RODE AWAY."

The boy looked anxiously at his mother, hoping she had not seen; but the gentle Lady was wringing her hands in distress. "Alas! alas!" she cried. "There has been a battle, and my Lord has sent home a prisoner. Oh, these weary, weary wars! Why can we not live in peace with our neighbors? Go you down, Alan, and see what word comes from my Lord!"

Alan ran hastily down; but when he reached the hall door the horsemen were no longer in sight. They must have turned aside into the bypath that led round to the south tower, under which the dungeons lay. Thither the boy hastened, down a winding path that led through the garden; but before he reached the south tower he saw one of the men-at-arms advancing toward him on foot.

"How now, Walter?" he cried. "What of my Lord? What has chanced? And who was yon on the gray mare?"

Walter of Welthorpe, a rough, grizzled man, doffed his cap respectfully to the Little Master.

"Good tidings, Master!" he said. "My Lord is well, and greets you and the Lady well. We have had good sport these days, young Sir; noble sport, truly; I would thou hadst been with us; but time enough for that."

"Oh! tell me, Walter, tell me!" cried Alan. "I will take you to my mother, but tell me as we go along, how fared it all?"

"Why, thus!" said Walter, well enough pleased to tell his tale. "The day we left, we came in over Ottercap Hill, and so down by Roddeley Crag. There met we with the Douglas, and with him the Lindsays and Graemes, and all the Gordons. When we came to Green Leyton the stags were leaping like hares in the bracken, and there we lighted down and went a-hunting. Twenty fat harts, as I am living man, we slew that day. Of these we of our party took three, and Giles and Chubby Dick are bringing of them back. But some part we roasted there, even under the brow of Ottercap, and there we feasted and were merry the better part of the night. So on the morn the Douglas felt the blood quick and lively in him, and he would go beard the Percy in his hall, and tempt him forth to battle. Some of the Graemes said him nay, they must be winning their hay while the season was good; base churls they were! But other of them would go with us, and every Gordon and Lindsay of them all. So on we rode, and on, and harried Bamborowe[4] as we went, and set the Otter Dale afire and left it burning. So when we came to Newcastle towers, the Douglas rode out before us all and called loud on the Percy by his name. 'Harry Percy,' quoth he, 'an thou bidest within, come to the field and fight!' And told him how we had burned and harried, and thought no more

4   Bamborough. A village in Northumberland, often mentioned in Border wars; celebrated for its castle founded about 547.

of him now than of Dick's red cow. A merry flouting was that; whatever is to come of it. Then came out the Percy on the walls, and a wrathful man was he. 'And for this,' he says, 'that thou hast done, Douglas, the one of us shall die before he lays by his armor.' So that, see ye, lad, was what the Douglas asked, nought else. 'So where shall I wait for thee?' he asks. 'Whatever place thou name, Percy,' he said, 'there shalt thou find me and mine.'

'And Harry Percy, go up to Otterbourne, and wait there three days, till my men are ready, and we will meet you there.'

Then both lords swore a great oath, so it should be; and we turned, and rode toward Otterbourne. But as we rode, even a league beyond Newcastle, we met a young fellow hawking, and he wore the Percy colors. A saucy spark he was, and would not answer, save that he was no Percy. His dress belying him, and no account to give of himself, my Lord would have made tree-fruit of him then and there, for there should be no spying and prying on our riding: but he minded him of certain things left behind, and so bade Rob and me ride for them, and take the lad and clap him in hold. So in hold he lies, Little Master, and there he may bide for me: but stay me not now, for I must mount and ride, ride, lest I miss the merry-making at Otterbourne yonder."

CHAPTER X

OTTERBOURNE

THERE was little mirth in Morven Castle that day and the next. Do what they would, all hearts were in the field with their Lord; all eyes were peering from the windows, watching for the first glint of steel or flutter of pennon round the curve of the road.

The second day was near its close. Alan was curled up in his favorite place on the broad window-seat of the great hall, Elspat beside him. The little girl had been very silent since her father went away. Her round cheeks were pale, and her blue eyes had a startled look as if she were listening and fearing what might befall. It was she who caught the first glimpse of something moving among the trees that arched over the roadway.

"Alan!" she cried, "Alan! they are coming! oh, look! look!"

The Little Master sprang to his feet, and looked eagerly where she pointed. Round the curve came a horseman, riding slow and wearily: then another, and another: and then no more. Of the twenty who had ridden out so gallantly from Morven, three returned, and of these three—

"Alan!" cried Elspat, "our father is not with them! First rides Dick Longbow, and then David—oh, good David! he will tell us all—and the third is Walter again: but where is our Lord Father?"

"Feasting with the Douglas, I'll warrant!" said Alan boldly, but his heart sank in spite of himself at the look of the little band.

They were now in full sight, riding heavily, with downcast looks. The Morven pennon, torn and stained, drooped from a broken shaft: the very horses seemed to tread mournfully, like the bearers of ill news.

Down ran the children to the hall door; down came the Lady, her trembling maids behind her, old Oona hobbling last on her stick: out came Duncan the steward, and Donald the falconer, and every soul alive in Morven Castle, and gathered round the silent group, the three down-looking men on the jaded horses.

"Speak, David Johnstone!" cried the Lady. "What tidings of my Lord? He is well? he is—tell me quickly, David! let me not wait, for good tidings or ill!"

David Johnstone dismounted, and knelt to kiss the Lady's hand. "My Lord lives!" he said quickly. "Many a Scottish knight lies dead beside Otterbourne this day, but my Lord of Morven lives."

"Now Heaven be praised!" cried the gentle Lady. "Alan! Elspat! oh, my bairns, all is well with your father; thank Heaven with me!"

"Nay! and alas! I said not so!" said the harper mournfully. "Living he is; for so much we may give true thanks; thankful may we be, too, that the victory lay with Scotland on the Day of Otterbourne—" A cry of joy broke from the listeners, but the harper checked them with a gesture. "Rejoice while you may!" he said. "But to speak all the truth is sad work for me. The Douglas is slain, and my Lord lies in prison in Newcastle[5] Tower."

Again a cry went up; but this time it was one of rage and sorrow. The men laid hands on their swords; the women trembled and clung about their Lady. She, gentle and timid in general, now stood up straight and white as a royal lily.

"David Johnstone," she said, "I see well that you have a heavy tale to tell, but you have ridden far and are weary men. Come into the hall and rest you, and while you rest, we will hear how things fell out, and what this is that hath chanced to my Lord."

5   Newcastle. The chief town of Northumberland. Its castle, built by the Normans in 1080 and rebuilt by Henry II, was a famous stronghold.

Calm and high she spoke, and those about her grew calm from her courage. Little Elspat stopped crying, and kissed her mother's hand as she clung to it, and Alan's head was held proudly as he handed his Lady mother into the castle hall.

Here, after Duncan had brought food and drink, David the Harper told his tale.

"'Twas on Wednesday, three days ago, that the Douglas pitched his camp at Otterbourne. It was late in the evening and we were weary men, so each lay down and slept beside his sword on the heather.

"Before dawn of the next day, while all our host lay in deep slumber, a lad came running to the Douglas in his tent. 'Awake, Douglas!' he cried, 'awake, for thine enemies are upon thee.'

"Lord James raised himself on his elbow as he lay. 'Now,' he said, 'if this be false, thou little lad, and thou hast broke my rest for nought, thou shalt hang on the highest tree in Otterbourne; but if it be true, shalt choose thy own reward. And true it well may be,' he said, 'for I have dreamed a dreary dream this night. I saw a dead man win a fight, and I think that man was I!' But still the lad cried, 'Awake, Douglas! the Percy is at hand, and seven standards with him.'

"Then up sprang every man and grasped the sword

that was by him, and made ready to fight, and before the sleep was well out of our eyes, here was the white lion banner of the Percy waving against the gray sky, and the English marching on Otterbourne[6], crying on St. George of England.

"We on our part cried on good St. Andrew,[7] and so to it we fell, sharp and swift. Arrows flew from our bows, piercing buff coat and baldrick, sword and axe were sharp and bright that tide, and bright the moon glanced on them, and on shining helm and target. Man to man we fought, Southron to Scot, and none asked quarter nor gave. Even so came the Douglas and the Percy together, and fought hand to hand, foot to foot, blade against bright blade. Then fire flashed and sparks flew from helm and harness; great battle was there before the dawn of the day. The Percy struck a mighty blow, which clove Lord James's helmet in two and dealt him a sore wound on the brow. He staggered back a pace and fell, and his men closed round to the rescue, but he would none of them save his own sister's son, Sir Hugh Montgomery. Then came Sir Hugh speedily and knelt down by his good Lord and asked his will.

"My nephew bold," said the Douglas, "what matters

6   St. Andrew. The patron saint of Scotland.
7   The battle of Otterburn, or Chevy Chase, was fought August 19th, 1388. See Percy's Reliques of Ancient English Poetry.

the death of one? The day is ours, full well I know, for I saw it in my dream. Now my wound is deep, and I fain would sleep. Lay me in the bracken bush that grows yonder, and tell none of my death, but cry the name of Douglas and it shall lead my merry men to victory. But bury me here on this lea, beneath the blooming brier, and let never mortal know that a kindly Scot lies here!"

"Ohon! and alas! no word more spoke the Douglas, but yielded up his soul to God. Bitter tears then wept the Montgomery, and I with him, for I was near at hand. We lifted up our noble lord, and laid him in the great bush of bracken that hid him from the sight of all; soft couch it was for those bold limbs that oft had lain on cold stone.

"Then Sir Hugh Montgomery lifted the Douglas his banner, and took the great sword from his side, and so to battle once more, crying his Lord's name. The moon shone clear, the day drew near, the Scottish spears made brave havoc through the English ranks. The Gordons steeped their hose and shoon in English blood; the Lindsays flew like fire about; it was a gallant fray. When the Montgomery found the Percy, he struck at him amain, and he at him again with great and mighty strokes; but Montgomery fought with dead hand on living, and soon the Percy was beaten to his knee. Sir Hugh cried on him to yield, but he, 'To whom shall I yield, if so it must be?'

"Thou shalt not yield to lord nor loon," said Sir Hugh, "but to the bush of bracken yonder."

"Not I!" cried the Percy, "only to the Douglas will I yield, or Montgomery if he were here."

Then Sir Hugh did off his helmet, and when the Percy knew him, he gave up his sword and owned himself captive. So ended that great fight on Otterbourne. The sun rose and shone on the dead of both sides; in thousands they lay, their faces upturned to the day, their wounds in front as became good men and true.

"But alas! for Morven that day! Our Lord was in such hot haste, pursuing certain of the foe as they fled, that he outrode our armies and Otterbourne to boot, his sole self chasing a whole troop, his heart the heart of ten. So fell they on another band of English, riding to rescue their own master if they might: but learning that all was over, and they too late for fight, they closed around our good Lord, and he, fighting like a lion, was still overcome of numbers, and borne away to Newcastle Tower, as I said in the beginning. So here endeth my tale, Lady and Master and good folks all, for the sorrow of Douglas and Morven, but the glory of Scotland while time shall last."

CHAPTER XI

THE CAPTIVE

"OH Alan!" cried little Elspat. "Alan, how 'tis as if the ballads were coming true. Did you hear how David told it, almost like a song? Ohon! and alas! what shall we do?"

The children had crept away to their own playroom, a small square room at the top of one of the high towers of the castle. It was little like the playrooms of to-day. There were two or three deerskins on the stone floor; a low table and a couple of creepies; Alan's bow and quiver hanging on the wall, some strings of birds' eggs neatly blown, a set of knucklebones made from the joints of a fish's backbone; this was really all, save for Elspat's little harp, the most precious thing she had in the world. David had brought it to her, and told her how it had belonged to a little Princess of Scotland who died; after her death her mother could not bear the sight of the harp; she gave it to the royal harper, and he to David, and he in turn to Elspat; so now she cherished Princess Fiona's harp, and loved it next to her mother and Alan. The Lady had made a silken cover for it, and it hung beside Alan's bow, the wonderful bow that the head forester, Red Jock Ogilvie, shaped for the boy with his own hands.

The children were sitting sad and sorrowful on their stools; Elspat weeping softly and drying her tears with her little kerchief, Alan looking moodily on the ground.

"The Douglas dead!" he said. "A black day for the Marches of Scotland!"

"And our Lord father in prison!" cried Elspat. "Oh, woful hour! To be shut up in a darksome den like—" she caught her breath suddenly. "Alan!" she cried. "Do you mind—oh, Alan! do you mind the stranger they brought home the other day?"

"Ay! I mind him!" said Alan briefly.

"Did they send him home, Alan, think you, or—" the little girl's voice faltered.

"Nay! they put him in the dungeon. I did not tell thee, Elsie; such things are not for little maids to know; but now that our own Lord lies in dungeon hold, we may be glad enough that our own castle rock holds one of the Percy band, black be the fall of them!"

The boy spoke fiercely, his dark eyes flashed; but little Elspat cried, "No! no! brother Alan! Not so does mother teach us. She says God hears the sighing of the prisoners; and if one, then another. If He hears our father, will He not hearken to the other poor man?"

"He is a Percy!" said Alan doggedly. "He is our enemy, and the enemy of our house."

"But—but—" cried the little girl, "he is there under ground, Alan! And no light coming in to him, and horrid things under his feet, and—oh, I canna bear to think of him."

"Dinna think of him, then!" said Alan.

"But I must: I canna keep it from me. Oh, Alan, lad, could we no let him out, you and me?"

"Elspat," said Alan sternly, "no more word of this! Our father left the castle in my charge; did ye no hear him? A pretty thing it would be for the Master of Morven to set free his Lord's prisoner, and he away and in hold himself. No more words, you silly lassie!"

"Only one word more will I say!" said little Elspat, "and that the word I said before, that the Lord God on high hears the sighing of the prisoners."

But it was a strange thing that chanced that night. The evenings were long and light, for it was summer. The Lady, worn out with weeping, had gone early to her bower, and old Oona had taken Elspat off early too, to the little airy room where their two pallets were spread.

Alan had sought out the harper, and the two friends were pacing slowly along the rough path that ran beneath the castle walls, round the whole circuit of the building.

The harper was telling over again the story of Otter-bourne, the boy listening with painful eagerness.

"Ay!" said David Johnstone. "Long the countryside will ring with the tale of this day—long, long will it ring. The bracken bush; ay! see you now, lad, that is a tale for a song; it is a song David will be making of it one day. Ay! ay! so the songs come to be. The bracken bush!"

He began to hum under his breath, trying this note and that, and fitting words to them the while. Presently, he unslung the harp that hung at his back and struck two or three chords softly; then suddenly threw back his head and sang in his deep clear voice:

> "But I have seen a dreary dream,
>   Beyond the isle o' Sky;
> I saw a dead man win a fight,
>   And I think that man was I."

"Oh, David!" cried Alan. "That is bonny! Oh, can ye not go on and tell!"

"Whisht now! whisht!" said the harper. "Dinna speak to a man when he's making a song. It must come of itself, man; it must come of itself."

Again he thrummed his harp, humming to himself; then again broke out in song:

"Two Little Hands Clasping The Bars Of A Grated Window."

> "My wound is deep, I fain would sleep,
>   Nae mair I'll fighting see;
> Go lay me in the bracken bush
>   That grows on yonder lea.
>
> But tell no one of my brave men
>   That I lie bleeding wan,
> But let the name of Douglas still
>   Be shouted in the van."

All this while they were pacing slowly along the walk; now they turned a sharp angle and came upon the dungeon keep, standing stark and black in the evening light. Alan stopped short with a low cry.

"What is yon?" he said in a trembling voice. "David, what is yon?"

At the foot of the grim black tower, a figure was crouching on the ground—a little white figure with golden hair. Two little hands clasping the bars of a grated window, a rosy face pressed against the grating—what was yon, indeed?

"Hist!" said the harper, in a low voice. "'Tis the little Lady!"

"*Elspat!*" cried Alan; and spite of David's caution, his voice rang out sharp in surprise and displeasure. At sound of it, the child started; then, springing to her feet, came running toward them with outstretched hands. "Oh, brother! oh, David!" she cried, "dinna flyte[8] me! He is no Percy, he says. He swears he is no Percy! Oh, listen to me, Alan!" For she saw in terror her brother's brow darken with one of the sudden rages that sometimes came over him. The boy's eyes flashed fire. "Elspat!" he cried. "You have not dared—you have never dared to speak to a prisoner! You, the daughter of Morven! Shame upon you! Shame!"

Anger choked his utterance, but David the harper laid a quiet hand over his mouth.

"If there is shame," he said gravely, "it is when the Master of Morven speaks roughly to his Lady sister. Keep Tom Tongue at home, boy, till he can speak fair and seemly. And come you here, my lily flower, and tell old David what has chanced, and how it is that this hour finds you kneeling by dungeon grates instead of at your sweet prayers within."

Leading the now sobbing child a little way apart, he sat down on a mossy rock; and taking her on his knee, signed to Alan to sit down beside him. The boy obeyed, his breast still heaving with anger; he dared not disobey the harper, who spoke with authority—and besides, spite of his rage, he wanted desperately to know what Elspat had heard.

8   *Flyte*; scold.

Soothed by David's kind words and voice, the little girl told her story: how she could not rest in her bed for thought of the poor captive in the dungeon; how she thought it could be no harm to take him a parcel of oat cakes and a cup of milk; thought it could be no harm to do what the good Lord Jesus said; and so—and so—he was hungry, woful hungry; and oh, David, 'tis sooth!" cried the child. "He is no Percy, but a Highland lad of the Graemes, taken by the Percys, and his father slain before his eyes, and his home burned. They forced him to wear their colors and serve them; he was biding his time till he should be old enough and strong enough to take his revenge and escape. Oh, David, he knows every crook and turn of Newcastle; if we let him free, he would help our Lord father to escape. He says—oh, Alan, listen to him, and dinna flyte me!"

CHAPTER XII

THE WHITE MAID OF NEWCASTLE

IN the Morven Castle of the morning, three people took the forest path that wound southward over moor and heath toward Newcastle. They were well mounted: David the harper on Strawberry, a powerful roan, old and wise. The Little Master rode his own Sultan, a beautiful little Arabian chestnut with a white star on his forehead, the pride of Alan's heart. Between them rode a youth of eighteen or thereabouts, clad in the Percy colors—a tall, slender lad, with fiery black eyes and a shock of tawny hair. He glanced about him with fierce, restless eyes; looking at him, Alan could think of nothing but a fettered hawk, chafing at the leash that held him.

Three went out, and three saw them go. From the postern gate, Evan Cameron the warder watched them, and shook his grizzled head. "Forty years I have kept watch and ward in Morven," he said, "and never till now saw I a prisoner loosed without ransom. I doubt I must answer for it with my head; yet David swears he will take all the blame; and how could I deny the Master of Morven when he laid his commands upon me, and spoke so like his father it shook the heart in me? I wish good may come of it, but I fear, I fear!"

But from the bower window, high in the north tower, the Lady and her little daughter, clasped in each other's arms, watched with beating hearts.

"My boy!" cried the gentle Lady. "Oh, my son! What if he be riding to his own death? Elsie, Elsie, why did we let him go?"

Little Elspat's eyes shone through the tears like blue stars.

"He will win through!" she cried. "He will win clear and bring my Lord father back safe and well. I know it, mother dear; I am as sure as if I saw them riding back even now. David is so wise, and so skilled in every device; and Nicol Graeme is true man, trust me but he is. He has a little sister—oh, mother, he knows not where she is since the black day when the Percys harried his glen. Oh, do you think when my father is home safe and well, he will help Nicol to find his little sister?"

"If he comes home safe and well!" sighed the Lady. "Surely he will, my little Elspat—if he comes!"

"Nay!" cried Elspat. "I said when!"

Riding over the wild moors, southward toward Newcastle, the Little Master, his anger clean forgot, chatted joyously with his prisoner. Always eager for new and strange things, he listened to tales of the Highlands, of glen and mountain and lake. The Highland lad told of his parents' death, his own capture, his patient biding the hour of revenge.

"And I think it dawns e'en now!" he said. "I think it dawns e'en now. The Percy prisoner, and Nicol Graeme free of foot, and bound to set him free—that may gar the red cock crow from Newcastle Tower. A blythe day for my father's son!"

"Nay! nay, lad! we'll have no red cocks crowing!" quoth David Johnstone. "I am a man of peace, and peaceful way must win this day. Now, as to this dungeon you tell of. It lies under a haunted tower, you say; and the spectre that walks is that of a maid in white?"

"Ay! the White Maid of Newcastle. She comes when danger bodes for the house of Percy, as I told you. The man her eye glances on will sicken of a fever, yet he may recover; the man her finger touches dies within the month."

"And they hold this for sooth in Newcastle Tower?"

"What else? It hath been proved, nor once only, but many times."

The Little Master looked doubtfully at the harper; David did not believe in ghosts, he knew, though most people did in those days. But in this case—The harper met his glance, and shook his head with a smile.

"Prove is a large word," he said; "but true or false, it suits our plan well this day. Listen, lads!"

It was night in Newcastle Tower. A sorrowful place it was, and had been ever since the day of Otterbourne. Their Lord, their great and glorious Harry Percy, was captive in Castle Dangerous. True, his foe and rival, James of Douglas, lay in a darker and narrower prison, his grave beside the bracken bush upon the lily lea; true also that a noble prisoner lay in their own dungeon, deep under the castle rock; but even these things could not lighten their hearts; and every brow was sad, from the Countess weeping in her silken bower to the sentinel on guard outside the door of the gloomy cell where the Baron of Morven lay.

It was cold in the prison gallery, cut out of the living rock. The lonely sentinel shivered in his buff jerkin, and beat his arms upon his breast as he walked slowly up and down. It was a dreary post. There was no light save that of his lantern set on the ground by the door of the cell he guarded, and that was dim and faint. On either hand the long narrow gallery melted into blackness. A dreary post indeed! Now and then the man paused in his walk, and peered uncertainly into the darkness, first one way, then the other.

"Black as a peat hag!" he muttered. "And this poor flicker only shows the darkness. Ugh! and cold as the grave. I would I were well out of this. Marry, and I should be, had they but given this Scot the steel in his vitals instead of on his wrists. They are all for ransom, ransom. Plain Jock gets a short shrift and a grave where he falls, if there be any to dig it for him; but when there is gold to be got, some poor fellow must freeze the marrow in his bones watching lest prisoner and ransom win free. Ugh! Baron or boor, I would ransom him with my pike's end, had I—"

"Hark! what is that?" A footstep sounded on the stone floor. The man caught up his pike. "Stand!" he cried. The sound ceased.

"Well!" said a voice. "I am standing. What next?"

"Who comes?" cried the soldier.

"A friend!"

"The password, friend, or back the way you come."

"Cockaleekie!" was the reply, in a half-laughing tone.

"No foolery!" said the soldier fiercely. "Who art thou, to come here at this time of night with thy quips and japes?"

"Who am I? why, a fool in good sooth, I believe. I

said 'Cockaleekie' because it was what brought me hither. Sniff with thy nose, and wilt smell it. Jess the kitchen maid met me e'en now as I was going to my bed, with a sad tale of a poor lad that was a friend of hers, and must mount guard this night in the dungeon gallery. He would be both cold and hungry, she said, and would I be a charitable soul and take him a mess of cockaleekie that she had kept hot for him between two covers? So being charitable, or a fool, or both being the same thing, I even took the dish and came, with no thought but to please the lass, who is a comely lass enough. But since I have no other password save my cockaleekie, I must e'en go back the way I came, as thou sayest."

The speaker, who was invisible in the blank darkness, began to move away. "Stay!" cried the sentry; "stay! art a good fellow, I'll warrant, and Jess is a thoughtful lass. After all, cockaleekie is a fair word for a hungry man, and I know not—who art thou? Advance, and let me have a look at thee!"

Nicol Graeme, for it was he, came forward into the dim circle of light cast by the lantern. He was holding a covered dish carefully in both hands. A savory steam came from it; the sentry sniffed eagerly. "It is thou, Nicol!" he cried; "why didst not say so? Beshrew thee for a Jack-o'-lantern as thou art! might'st have lost me my supper, and I in such need of it as never man was before. Give it here!"

He took the dish eagerly, and squatting down with it between his knees, began to eat as if he were famished indeed. Nicol Graeme watched him in silence.

Cockaleekie is a Scottish dish, chicken and bacon, peas and carrots and onions all cooked together into a savory stew: the hungry soldier smacked his lips as he ate.

"'Tis a brave dish!" he said with his mouth full. "And she was a brave lass that sent it."

"Ay! and what about me that brought it?" asked Nicol. "Methinks I was a brave lad, and a bold one, to come this way after what Jess was telling me."

"And what was that?" The sentry looked up in some alarm.

"Nought new to you most like, but I had not heard; that the White Maid walks in Newcastle these nights."

"Who said it? Who hath seen her? Where—" The soldier scrambled to his feet, and his glance darted right and left down the black gloom of the gallery. "Who hath seen her?" he cried again. "Where does she walk?"

"I dinna mind," said Graeme carelessly. "Old Simon; was it old Simon she looked on? Ay, it was, and he lies stricken with fever since he saw her last night."

"Where?" asked the soldier again. "Where did he see her?"

"In the long gallery, or so Jess had it. 'Tis in the galleries she ever walks, they say. Who is it you guard here, friend Will? A prisoner of Otterbourne?"

"Ay! a Scottish noble, he of Morven: held for ransom, and for pledge of our own good Lord. The worse luck for me! I would I were out of this place!"

"Morven!" repeated the Highland lad. "I met a man of Morven on the road not long syne; a minstrel he was, and he played me a tune on his harp; a bonny tune. How went it, now? I mind me—" He whistled a bar or two of a lively air, but broke off suddenly. "What—" he said, and his voice faltered—"what is that, Will?" As he spoke he pointed over the other's shoulder. The soldier turned hastily, and both stared down the long passage to the left. The blackness of darkness—was it? Or was something glimmering pale against the black? Something that fluttered, vanished, appeared again; finally came slowly and steadily towards them. A white figure, tall and slender, wrapped in a veil or mantle; the face hidden; one hand extended, the forefinger pointing— The soldier clutched Graeme's arm for a moment, staring with parted lips and eyes starting from their sockets; then with a wild scream, "The White Maid!" he rushed headlong in the opposite direction. There was the sound of a scuffle, a groan, a fall. "Hither, lads!" said a low voice. Nicol Graeme ran forward; the white figure followed, casting off its veil as it ran. They found David Johnstone kneeling on the prostrate soldier, one hand pressed firmly over his mouth.

"Quick!" he said; "tear a strip from thy mantle, Master, and give it me for a gag; so! now the cords; tie me his ankles; now his wrists; so! there we have him, and a pretty piece of work as one need see. Now for his keys! Quiet, lad, quiet, and no harm shall come to thee!" For the unhappy sentinel, stunned at first by his fall, was coming to himself, and struggling to free himself of his bonds. "Quiet, I say, and no harm shall come to thee; but make a sound, and there shall need no White Maid of Newcastle to tell thee that thine hour has struck."

"Where is the door, Graeme?" Graeme raised the lantern, and showed a low door in the wall, heavily barred with iron. "Master, take thou the keys!" said the harper. "Thou and no other shalt set free thy father."

"And I," said Nicol Graeme, "will e'en sit me down and finish the cockaleekie; 'twere a pity to waste good food, and I fear me friend Will here hath lost his appetite."

CHAPTER XIII

ALL'S WELL!

"BUT how did ye get in?" asked the Baron of Morven.

Four were riding along the road where three had ridden, but in the opposite direction. Swiftly they rode, and joyfully, though ever and anon an anxious glance was cast backward to see if they were pursued. It was still dark, though the east began to show gray where the dawn was to come.

"How did ye get in?" asked the Baron.

"'Twas David planned it all, father!" cried Alan eagerly. "David and Nicol, 'tis them we have to thank this night."

"Tush!" said the harper. "Modesty is a pretty thing, in youth especially, but truth comes first, and we should have been ill off without our Little Master this night. To say all, my Lord, it took the three of us to play the play; nay, four, for where should we have been without my harp?"

He touched his harp lovingly as he spoke.

"'Twas this opened the gate to me!" he said. "I stood outside and began to sing, and they soon had me in. When they found I was at Otterbourne, they came round me like bees round a honey-tree, and twice and thrice I must sing the song; and while I sang and they listened, craning their necks and stretching their ears, the two lads crept in through a postern that Graeme knew of, and so into the castle. "And here they wellnigh came to shipwreck on the very threshold, for as Nicol led the way he ran into one of the household who was making his own way out to take his pleasure, without leave asked or given. See now, my Lord, how young wits work! Before the fellow could speak, Nicol was on his neck crying to him to save him, save him, for death was on his heels. Held him there, mark you, crying and moaning, while our Little Master undid the bundle and wrapped the white veil round him. "Then—tell you, Nicol; I saw not this part."

"I hung on his neck," said the Highland lad, "till I caught a flutter of white with the tail of my eye. Then I gave a skriegh and jammed him against the wall and held him there, the two of us groaning and shaking, while the White Maid of Newcastle gaed by. Lad, but that was a fearsome look ye gied us. It garred my blood run cold, and I knowing you; but poor Simon! When you glowered at him and raxed out your hand I thought the soul would leave his body with fear."

"But I didna touch him!" cried Alan eagerly. "I didna

touch him, father, to have maybe his death at my door. David has known men die of fright, he says. I only rolled my eyes at him and clawed the air a bit, and gurgled in my throat, and then on past him till I came to the hiding hole that Nicol told me of. "And then you—go on, Nicol!"

"Him and me," said Nicol, chuckling, "poor Simon and me, we stood clutching each ither and the wall till the boy was well out of sight, and then away with us out of the postern head over heels, merry-come-tumble, and never drew breath till we were in the castle kitchen.

"There we told our tale five times running, and by the fifth time the Maid was seven feet tall, with eyes of red fire, and where her robe brushed past Simon his side was all cold and dead-like, except for prickings as of a red-hot needle; and with that he took to his bed, and I to make love to Jess the cook maid for a mess of cock-aleekie. Sooth, I was better off than the Master here, who must bide in hiding hole till he should hear me whistle the 'Morven Merrymaking.'"

"Or than I," said the harper, "who must fret my heart out with wondering how it fared with you two, till I had the wit to ask for food, and so made my way to the kitchen. Thy grinning face was all the supper I needed, Nicol; I might have known thou wouldst be where food was."

"Thou might'st well!" said the Highland lad calmly. "I was aye hungry, most times since I can remember."

"Shalt never be hungry again, lad," said the Baron, "while there is meat in Morven. Wilt take service with me, Nicol Graeme?"

"Ay will I, my good Lord!" said Nicol. "Hand and foot I'll serve thee, and ride the Border side with thee when next thou seekest the Percy, in open field or in moated tower."

"And thou, Master of Morven, what sayest thou? Wilt ride the Border with me?"

"Oh, father!" cried Alan, and again, "Oh, father!" He could find no words, but his glowing cheeks and shining eyes spoke for him.

"Thou art over young to be knighted," said the Baron, "otherwise hadst won thy spurs this night; but thy father's page thou well mayst be, and shalt."

Alan tried to stammer his thanks, but the Baron laid his mailed hand on his shoulder a moment. "I know all thou wouldst say, lad!" he said, and there was that in his stern voice that Alan had never heard there before. "I know all thou wouldst say, but we Morvens have few words. Thou and these two have saved my life this night, and I do not forget. "But look! yonder is the dawn, and yonder the first glimpse of bonny Morven: fair fall the towers of it!"

Alan looked, and there, sure enough, in the faint pearly morning light, was the grim castle, lifting its turrets above the clustering trees. Gazing eagerly, the boy saw something white at one of the upper windows.

"Oh, my Lord!" he cried. "Oh, father, they are at the window; they are watching, mother and Elsie, and Oona too. Mother said she should be watching from the first streak of dawn. I said if all was well I would wave my kerchief as I came round the turn. May I ride on, father, and give the good news?"

"Ride on, son of mine!" said the Baron. "Ride on, and mayst thou ever be the bearer of good news, Master of Morven!"

A touch of the spur, a whispered word; the Arab shot forward like an arrow, and with beating heart, with happy, shining eyes, his white kerchief waving on high, the Little Master rode on to carry the good news.

THE END